ELIZABITE

ADVENTURES OF
A CARNIVOROUS PLANT

by

H. A. REY

Houghton Mifflin Company
Boston

Library of Congress Cataloging-in-Publication Data

Rey, H. A. (Hans A.)
Elizabite: adventures of a carnivorous plant
Summary: Elizabite, an unusual Venus flytrap, bites everything
in sight and finally wins fame by capturing a burglar.
RNF ISBN 0-395-97702-9   PAP ISBN 0-395-97704-5
[1. Carnivorous plants — Fiction. 2. Stories in rhyme] I. Title.
PZ8.3.R325EL   1990
[E]   90-4834

Manuactured in the United States of America
WOZ 10 9 8 7 6 5 4

TO

PEGGY

YOU would not think that plants like meat.
Well, some plants do. They catch and eat
Small insects, such as flies and ants,
And they are called

CARNIVOROUS PLANTS.

One of them came to world-wide fame;
ELIZABITE, that was her name.

Elizabite smiles at the sky
While a mosquito passes by.

Right in the middle of its flight
She captures it with great delight.

Elizabite smiles at the sky . . .
There comes another passer-by.

It's Doctor White, a scientist,
And well-known as a botanist.

"This plant is very rare indeed!
I'll take her home and get the seed."

"She's caught me—Ouch!" cries Doctor White,
"I did not know this plant could bite."

He now tries out a safer way,
And he succeeds without delay.

Victorious he leaves the place,
A smile of triumph on his face.

Here in the doctor's laboratory
Continues the amazing story.

The plant, for once, behaves all right.
She gets a drink from Doctor White,

And even, as a special treat,
Frankfurters, for she's fond of meat.

But Scotty thinks with jealousy,
Frankfurters should belong to ME!

Alas, it never pays to steal!
Elizabite will spoil his meal.

A sudden snap—a cry—a wail—
And there goes Scotty minus tail!

Mary, the maid, comes with her broom
To tidy up the messy room

And, unsuspecting, turns her back:
A tempting aim for an attack!

Elizabite's bad deeds require
A solid fence of strong barbed wire.

And Doctor White reports the case
Now to Professor Appleface.

But Appleface declares, "I doubt it
Till I myself find out about it."

He soon obtains the evidence
Despite the new barbed wire fence.

"We have to keep Elizabite

Chained to the kennel now," says White.

This burglar does not realize
The danger of his enterprise . . .

Next morning White perceives with fright
Someone inside Elizabite!

"How brave of her to catch this man!
Let's put him in the prison van."

Of course, Elizabite can't stay
With White. She now is on her way

To a new home, the nearby Zoo.

Here she became—and this is true—

At once the most outstanding sight.
Surrounded by her children bright
She lived in happiness and glory
Up to this day...

Here ends the story.